my beak
book belongs
to

....

melanie walsh

my beak, your beak

Houghton Mifflin Company
Boston 2002

Dachshunds are long with little legs.

Dalmatians are tall and spotty. But...

they both love
chasing sticks!

grrrr

Sharks swim in the deep ocean.

Goldfish swim
in a bowl.
But...

glub!

they both
blow bubbles!

Penguins live in
the snowy South Pole

Robins live in your back yard. But...

they both have
pointy beaks!

yum

Lions are big and
have hairy manes.

Kittens are small and fluffy.

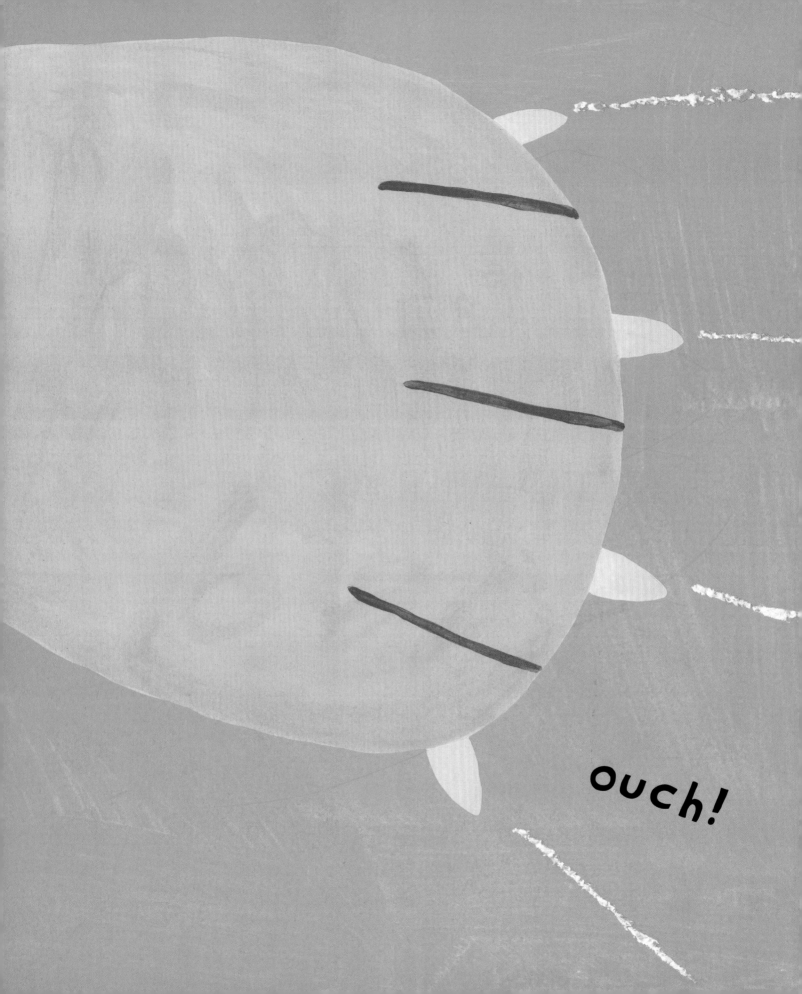

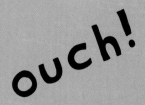

ouch!

they both have
scratchy claws!

Bush babies sleep in trees.

Bats sleep in
dark caves
But...

they're both
wide awake at night!

goodnight!